Williams, Garth.

Benjamin's treasure.

BENJAMIN'S TREASURE

Story and pictures by

Garth Williams

Watercolors by Rosemary Wells

HarperCollins *Publishers*

Benjamin Pink lived with his wife, Emily, in a little white house on Clover Hill. One bright summer morning Ben looked at the sky, and the sky was clear and blue. He looked at the sea, and the sea was smooth and green. "A perfect day for fishing!" said Ben. After breakfast, Ben went into the garden to dig up a worm.

PINK

Soon he had a good worm and his basket was full of lettuce and radish sandwiches. “I do think you should take a raincoat,” Emily called as Ben opened the garden gate.

“On a day like this?” said Ben. “Why, there’s not a cloud in the sky.” He looked up to make sure he was right. Then he promised to catch a great fish for dinner and, waving good-bye to Emily, he walked down the hill to the sea.

Down at the water Ben pushed his boat out into the open and rowed in the direction of Cape Hare. He looked up at the little white house on Clover Hill and waved. Emily waved back. "I really must catch a beautiful fish," said Ben to himself. "She deserves only the best."

When he was out near Cape Hare, Ben put the worm on his hook, cast his line into the sea, and opened up his lunch. Then he settled back for a calm day at sea. Ben sat there a long time. The line remained perfectly still.

It was a few hours later when Ben felt a drop of water hit the top of his ear and trickle down inside. He turned around and sure enough, a large blanket of dark clouds covered the sky behind him.

Just then he felt a violent tug—"A bite!" He started winding in his line, but he could hardly hang on. "This fish must be enormous," said Ben, leaning back as far as he could. He had to twist and turn and climb back and forth.

By now the rain was pelting down, but the fish still hung on. Suddenly Ben's foot caught in the strap of his lunch basket, and he slipped on the wet wooden seat of the boat. The fish pulled harder. A wave rose and covered Ben's head.

This was too much! He let the rod go and pulled himself back into the boat.

Then the storm cleared as quickly as it had come. The waves crept under the sea, and it was calm again. Ben put down his oars and looked around. He expected to see cliffs and his house, but all around him there was nothing but the sea and the darkening sky. He knew he was very far from home.

Suddenly a voice cried, “Hullo!” Ben looked up and saw a seagull sailing away toward something, something like the top of a tree and maybe a little land. Ben rowed toward it faster and faster.

Crash! "Ah! Oh! Whew!" gasped Ben. It was nearly dark, and he had hit a rock. His boat was in smithereens. At least he was on land. Ben crawled onto the beach and fell asleep to the sounds of the waves rolling onto the rocks.

In the morning Ben woke up on a desert island. His boat was just a few scattered boards. He wondered how he would ever get home to Emily. "While I am here I suppose I must make myself a house," he said. Soon earth was flying out from under Ben's bushy tail.

After a few hours of digging, Ben stopped to eat some berries. Just then he saw a ship going over the horizon. "Hi! Help!" he shouted as he dashed to the top of the hill. "Hi! Help!" Ben jumped up and down, but nobody could see a rabbit that far away.

Even more worried than before, Ben went back to digging his house. "I'll dig a cupboard in this corner," he said, "for food in case a storm blows up."

Suddenly his paw scratched against a hard lump just where his cupboard was to be. It was no rock. "Jumping radishes!" cried Ben. "Treasure!"

He could not believe his eyes and pulled his whiskers to be sure he was not dreaming. He dipped his paw into the chest and pulled out diamonds, gold, rubies, and pearls. Ben's knees were trembling. "There is so much treasure in here, Emily can have anything she wants."

Ben's excitement grew. "I shall buy presents for everyone on Clover Hill. A larger hospital, a new playground, free lettuce for the needy. Perhaps they will make me governor!"

Ben was so pleased he started practicing his governor's speech.

After three days Ben had a cozy home and a hiding place for his treasure. He built a bonfire on the hill to attract any ships that passed by. Every day he sat on top of his house and looked out to sea, but no one passed the island. He longed to get back to Emily.

One morning Ben noticed a peculiar-looking rock moving in the shallow water. When he went down to investigate, an old head popped out of the rock. "Good morning," said the turtle. "I am Theodore the Turtle." Ben shook the turtle's flipper.

“What a welcome surprise,” Ben said. “I had just lost hope of ever seeing anyone alive out here.” While they drank some mint tea and ate berries, Ben told Theodore the whole story of the storm and his new house.

“You are not very big,” said Theodore. “I might be able to take you home on my back.”

“I should very much like to try it,” said Ben, though he wondered if Theodore would be able to take the treasure as well. “But I have a secret to tell you.”

"You see," said Ben. "I have found a treasure here, and if you can rescue me, I will give you half." But Theodore did not look surprised.

"Oh, that," said the turtle. "I remember the day when the chest arrived. I was three hundred years younger than I am today. A boat ran up onto the sand, and in it was a group of buccaneers. It was a scruffy, rough, and barbarous crew. They buried the chest and never came back for it. If I were you, I would forget all about that treasure. You will worry about it day and night. Your friends will become jealous, and you will suspect everyone. You will worry what to spend it on or how to give it away."

But Ben did not want to give up his great plans to make things on Clover Hill better. "Well," said the turtle, "I suppose you won't be happy unless you can get home with your treasure. And since I cannot carry it, I shall ask my friend the porpoise to tow you, but you must make a good raft."

Then the turtle glided away in the water and disappeared in the deep shadows under the sea. Ben felt very lonely again. "I do hope he doesn't forget," he said to himself. He went back to his house and started to look for things to make a raft.

Ben worked hard from dawn until dark to make his raft. He collected all the wood he could find. At the end of the day he had all the pieces ready. The next morning he waded out into the sea and pulled long ribbons of seaweed. He cut long pieces with the edge of a shell to bind the sides around the raft. Ben was exhausted when he fell asleep that night.

The next day, when Theodore came back, Ben was eager to test out the raft. He emptied all the treasure out onto the floor and ran down the beach with a crown on his head and the empty chest. The turtle laughed at Ben, but Ben lifted the crown off, put it in the trunk with some gold bars, and started loading up the raft.

The raft began to creak louder and louder, and then one of the bars sank through the floor and disappeared. The raft was low in the water, and Ben was worried. He did not think he would get very much of his treasure home after all.

When the turtle turned to go, the sun was setting and most of the treasure was still on the floor of Ben's house. So Ben gathered it back into the cupboard and covered the hole with dirt. Then he curled up and fell asleep.

The next morning a very big porpoise came leapfrogging through the water. "Well, well," he said in a deep, gurgling voice. "You're the shipwrecked friend of Mr. Turtle. Let's go!"

Ben waded into the water and threw the porpoise his seaweed rope.

"Looks like a lovely storm coming," said the porpoise. It did look stormy. Ben was not happy about the idea of a rough sea, but it was too late.

"Isn't this rain fun?" said the porpoise. But Ben pulled the lid of the trunk over his head and tried to sleep to the pounding of the waves.

It didn't seem like very long before the porpoise called, "You're home!"

Ben couldn't believe it. He opened his trunk and looked out. But there was no Clover Hill and no little white house. Most of all, there was no Emily.

"This isn't home!" he shouted. But the porpoise was already gone. Around him danced about twenty monkeys, already playing with his treasure. They threw diamonds and pelted each other with rubies. They took pieces of his raft. By the time Ben climbed out, there was nothing left but a few sticks.

"The porpoise has made a dreadful mistake," wailed Ben. He tried to sit on the few twisted branches of raft that remained, but he was too heavy. So Ben made a ring out of what was left and stepped into it. "Better to have a life belt than nothing," he said, and he swam out into the sea.

Ben hoped he would see the turtle or the porpoise again. He had no idea which way to swim. "I shall never be seen again!" he sobbed. "Poor Emily, poor, poor Emily."

Just then there was a ripple in the water ahead. A black fin stuck out of the water and circled round him. In the dim moonlight Ben could see the shape of a large, long fish. "Excuse me," said Ben. "Can you help a fellow in a nasty fix?"

"Sure," said the fish. "Call me Sharky. Hold on!" and in a flash they were off at a terrific speed.

Soon Ben began to recognize the coast. Then he saw his little house on the hill. "That's it!" Ben shouted, and as quickly as he could thank the shark, Ben was running up the hill and into Emily's arms. It took hours to tell Emily his story, and Ben wasn't sure she believed him. But that night, when Ben fell, exhausted, into his own bed, Emily noticed something shining from inside Ben's ear. It was one of those pearls, still stuck there after all those miles.

In the morning Ben took Emily down to the sea.

"What is it?" asked Emily as Ben pointed toward the horizon.

"Over there, farther than you can see, is our treasure," he said.

"And when we have a proper sailing boat," said Emily, "we shall be sailing off together to collect it."

"Yes," said Ben. "But haven't I told you? I already have the most valuable treasure in the world."

"You do?" said Emily.

"Yes, right here," said Ben. "It is you, Emily."

When I was little there was one artist who charmed me in every book. It was Garth Williams. His was an unfailing instinct for how a character should look and exactly what moment in the text to illustrate. My respect for his artistry grew as I became an illustrator myself. I believe Garth Williams and Maurice Sendak are the two great geniuses of twentieth-century illustration in America.

This picture book was gleaned from *The Adventures of Benjamin Pink*, a story that Garth wrote and illustrated in 1951. It has been shortened to make it picture-book length, but every word is the author's own.

Reproducing his black-and-white halftone art in gentle color was the greatest challenge. Happily the original illustrations were found in pristine condition in a vault in Texas. We reproduced them in light gray ink on heavy Windsor & Newton handmade watercolor stock. Each drawing was then colored using the exact paints Garth had available to him in the fifties, in a palette chosen from his color work in other books.

This experience has been a labor of love for me. I welcome this opportunity, with the help of the editors and production staff at HarperCollins, to bring back some of this great genius's work for a new generation of readers.

ROSEMARY WELLS

Benjamin's Treasure The story and illustrations adapted for *Benjamin's Treasure* were originally published in novel form in *The Adventures of Benjamin Pink*, written and illustrated by Garth Williams. www.harperchildrens.com

Library of Congress Cataloging-in-Publication Data
Williams, Garth. Benjamin's treasure / Garth Williams ; illustrated by Rosemary Wells.
p. cm. Based on: The adventures of Benjamin Pink. Summary: A rabbit gets stranded on a deserted island with a trunk full of treasure and must find his way home. ISBN 0-06-028740-3 — ISBN 0-06-028741-1 (lib. bdg.)
[1. Rabbits—Fiction. 2. Buried treasure—Fiction.] I. Wells, Rosemary, ill. II. Adventures of Benjamin Pink.
III. Title. PZ7.W659 Be2001 00-40901 [E]—dc21

Typography by Carla Weise
1 2 3 4 5 6 7 8 9 10
❖
First Edition